Reycraft Books
55 Fifth Avenue
New York, NY 10003

Reycraftbooks.com

Text © 2021 Johnny Ray Moore
Illustration © 2021 Cbabi Bayoc

All rights reserved. No portion of this book may be reproduced, stored in a retrieval
system, or transmitted in any form or by any means, electronic, mechanical, photocopying,
recording, or otherwise, without written permission from the publisher.
For information regarding permission, please contact info@reycraftbooks.com.

Educators and Librarians: Our books may be purchased in bulk for promotional,
educational, or business use. Please contact sales@reycraftbooks.com.

This is a work of fiction. Names, characters, places, dialogue, and incidents
described either are the product of the author's imagination or are used fictitiously.
Any resemblance to actual persons, living or dead, is entirely coincidental.

Sale of this book without a front cover or jacket may be unauthorized. If this book
is coverless, it may have been reported to the publisher as "unsold or destroyed"
and may have deprived the author and publisher of payment.

Library of Congress Control Number: 2021902053

ISBN: 978-1-4788-7239-9

Printed in Dongguan, China. 8557/0421/17800

10 9 8 7 6 5 4 3 2 1

First edition hardcover published by Reycraft Books 2021

Reycraft Books and Newmark Learning, LLC, support diversity and
the First Amendment, and celebrate the right to read.

REYCRAFT
BOOKS

Seasonal Adventures

by Johnny Ray Moore

illustrated by Cbabi Bayoc

To my handsome grandson, Ethan O'Bryan Young;
my darling granddaughter, Jade Olivia Young;
and all children, near and far —J.R.M.

This is dedicated to my three children, and I hope they know I will be by their side through every season they experience. —Cbabi Bayoc

Welcome to Spring!

Tireless tadpoles
Swim with ease.

North Wind gently
Combs the trees.

Green grass growing
On a hill
Newborn, chirping
Whippoorwills.

Ravens cawing
In the wind
Dogwoods dressed
With leaves, again.

Quails astir
About the field
Amongst the shrubs
Are daffodils.

April showers
Somewhat soon
Cloudless skies, again,
By noon.

Life's anew
With sounds unheard
All because
Spring has occurred.

Welcome to

Summer!

Sunrays dancing

Ponies prancing

Kittens on their mother's back.

Frogs all hoppy

Puddles sloppy

Ducks are going

QUACK!
QUACK!
QUACK!

Thunder crashing
Lightning flashing
Raindrops cooling thirsty Earth.

People cheering
Dusk appearing
Runners racing
To be first.

Daisies blooming
Cats assuming
Dogs are sleeping
On the lawn.

Daylight fading
Cows parading
Back to shelter
At the barn.

Welcome to
SUMMER!

Welcome to
Fall!

Mornings with
A bit of chill
Jack Frost sprinkled
Down the hill.

Stacks of hay
All turning brown
Lined so neatly
On the ground.

Farmers plowing
Fields now bare
Leaves all scattered
Here and there.

Acorns from
The mighty oak
Chimneys coughing
Puffs of smoke.

Supper at
The brink of dusk
Plates all filled
With just enough.

Twinkling stars
At evening's end
Let us know
Fall now begins.

Welcome to FALL!

Mice are searching
In the earth
Lone wolf howls
For all it's worth.

Furry bunnies
Near a cave
Watching chipmunks
Misbehave.

Reindeer nosy
With their stares
Snoring, fuzzy
Wuzzy bears.

Leaves of color
Scattered 'round
Covering tracks
Upon the ground.

Gliding geese
Against the sun
Another season's
Just begun.

Welcome to Winter!

MEET
Johnny Ray Moore

Johnny Ray Moore is a poet, children's book author, greeting cards writer, and songwriter. He wrote his first poem when he was in the third grade. Johnny is a graduate of the Institute of Children's Literature and a member of the Society of Children's Book Writers and Illustrators. He lives in Knightdale, North Carolina, with his wife and one of their three daughters.

MEET Cbabi Bayoc

Cbabi (pronounced *Kuh-bob-bi*) Bayoc is an artist living in St. Louis, Missouri. His work has been described as unique, bold, and colorful, while adding some "phunk." Bayoc, whose given name is Clifford Miskell, Jr., adopted his name CBABI (Creative-Black-Artist-Battling-Ignorance) during his time at Grambling State University. BAYOC (Blessed-African-Youth-Of-Creativity) provided a unique and deep connection that would one day be shared with his children. Cbabi has created artwork for Prince, Muhammad Ali, and *Rap Pages* magazine, and his murals can be seen all over St. Louis. He is well known for his *365 Days with Dad* series, which paints a positive image of Black fatherhood.

WITHDRAWN